AT THE
CENTER

bOUNCE

AT THE
CENTER

PATRICK JONES

darbycreek

MINNEAPOLIS

Darby Creek
A division of Lerner Publishing Group, Inc.
241 First Avenue North
Minneapolis, MN 55401 USA

For reading levels and more information, look up this title at
www.lernerbooks.com.

Front cover: © istockphoto.com/MistikaS; Susan Rouleau-Fienhage (background).

Main body text set in Janson Text LT Std 12/17.5.
Typeface provided by Adobe Systems.

Library of Congress Cataloging-in-Publication Data

Names: Jones, Patrick, 1961– author.
Title: At the center / by Patrick Jones.
Description: Minneapolis : Darby Creek, [2016] | Series: Bounce | Summary: "When an African American student transfers from an inner-city basketball team to the suburbs, tension among the players and the coach erupts along racial lines. To the anger of his teammates, the coach kicks him off the team after he gets into a fight. Can a social media movement get him back on the court?"— Provided by publisher.
Identifiers: LCCN 2015041821| ISBN 9781512411225 (lb : alk. paper) |
    ISBN 9781512412062 (pb : alk. paper)
Subjects: | CYAC: Basketball—Fiction. | African Americans—Fiction. | Race relations—Fiction. | High schools—Fiction. | Schools—Fiction.
Classification: LCC PZ7.J7242 Atm 2016 | DDC [Fic]—dc23

LC record available at http://lccn.loc.gov/2015041821

Manufactured in the United States of America
1 – SB – 7/15/16

Thanks to the real Lucy for reading and recommending an earlier version, and to Judith Klein for her copyediting skills.

FRIDAY NIGHT
DECEMBER 2
Vestavia Hills (Alabama) High School gym

Even sitting all comfy at the end of the bench, far away from the action, I hear the loud smack as Jayson's fist smashes into the jaw of the big, white, doofus center from Mountain Brook High who'd been elbowing him all night. No doubt under Jayson's number 45 uniform, his light brown skin is covered with dark blue bruises. The doofus gets not one, but two shots. *Bam bam*. So in addition to Jayson's first-half triple-double, add another double: two fists to the face.

The home crowd goes wild. It's huge because there's not much else to do in Vestavia Hills on a Friday night. Players from both teams converge on the fight. Bench-sitters like me leap off the pine like it's on fire. Everybody's man-on-man except the doofus, who is man-on-floor. It's a crazy scene, and I jump into it with enthusiasm, which I have more of than basketball skills. Being on the court, like I am now, is something I've only experienced once—and only for two minutes—in our team's first two games. Games we won easily because of Jayson "Dominator" Davis.

Jayson stands over his fallen foe big as a house until our coach, blue eyes bulging and square jaw sticking out, grabs Jayson by the back of his jersey and spins him around. Coach gets in Jayson's face, which means he needs to stand on his toes since Jayson is six ten and Coach isn't even close. Coach gets up in his ears too. I can't hear it, but I can see the pained expression on Jayson's face. One part's disappointment and the other part's anger. Something you learn early in sports is that the coach is always right, even when he's wrong. Jayson, my best friend on the team, has burned with anger toward Coach since transferring to Vestavia High at the start of the year. He's a black barracuda in an ocean of whitefish.

The refs blow their whistles like steam engines to calm things down. The players retreat to their benches so we can continue the game to the inevitable conclusion: another Vestavia Hills victory. Or maybe not, because I hear the ref with gray hair eject Jayson, but not the downed doofus-tree. I wait for Coach to argue it. Instead he pushes Jayson away from the floor—two hands hard on the number 45—except Jayson's not moving. It's one on one: two hundred–plus pounds of young muscle versus thirty years of old-school coaching. Who wins?

"I've had it with your ghetto court crap!" Coach yells for the top row to hear. Coach might know basketball, but he doesn't know anything about men. If he did, he wouldn't treat Jayson, A.C., and Gerald like second-class citizens. I guess since I'm even lighter-skinned than the over-tanned white girls and since I run his stupid plays, unlike the three other black kids on the team, that's why Coach isn't on my case.

Jayson doesn't say much, as usual. His head's down, his tense face filled with sweat, as he takes Coach's verbal beat-down. It goes on and on until Coach calls Jayson "a thug." Jayson's head snaps up. "What'd you say?"

Coach answers like he does almost all our questions: with stone-cold silence.

Then Coach booms, "Say another word and you're suspended for two games, not one. Got it?"

Jayson drops his head, then scans the scene, measuring the team. He's got some friends, like me, A.C., and Gerald, but more enemies, like Lex. Jayson lifts his head, winks, and says, "Word."

"That's two. Want it to be three?"

While I've never hit a three in my court career, I can stop one. I bound from the bench he got pulled because he broke another rule (didn't run Coach's prehistoric plays). Last game, he got benched because he broke rule three: taking three-pointers. He made 'em, but that's not how Coach plays the game. He plays "ball control offense" like he must have done it in the dinosaur days: slow and stupid.

"What do you think?" I ask A.C. He's the smartest person I know, other than my girl, Lucy. In front of us, Gerald sighs heavily. The game's on his shoulders now. "So, A.C., what—"

A.C. gives me a "Whatcha gonna do?" shrug and says nothing. As I watch the game slipping away, even though Gerald and the others are running Coach's plays just like he put 'em on the blackboard, I wonder what's gonna happen to Jayson, number 45, sitting for two games.

At the half, we return to the locker room. Coach follows us, ranting and grumbling and not acknowledging the key player he just benched. Finally, I just ask, "When is Jayson coming back?"

Coach stares me down, then clears his

throat like it's full of razor blades but doesn't answer my question.

"We're in this together," I whisper to A.C. and Gerald.

"Like peas in a pod, Cody?" Gerald asks me.

I cover my mouth with my hand, then mumble the answer: "Yeah, black-eyed peas."

Gerald snickers, which causes me to laugh, then A.C. busts a gut instead of acting all sad because we're losing a game that doesn't really matter. Eyes flash red at us with anger. We're in Alabama, but us three, we might as well be from another planet.

rose in the west and set in the east. They hold hands until the bell rings. People get quiet pretty quickly in this class, more so than in any other, since Mr. Austin actually holds our attention and respect.

"Today we're beginning a unit on civil disobedience, something close to my heart."

"That's because you were a hippie!" Danni shouts.

Mr. Austin shakes his head, laughs. "Danni, the only thing I was protesting in the days of the hippies was not getting more time for recess," Mr. Austin says. "I didn't grow up in the 1960s, but this country sure did."

"Especially here," Danni adds. I nod in agreement. Birmingham was ground zero for the civil rights movement. A lot of good stuff happened here, like the Birmingham Children's Crusade, but more bad, like those young girls getting killed in a church bombing on Christmas morning in 1963. I guess they needed both good and bad to make the movement work. Only thing is, all the stuff they protested against back in the day seems to me hasn't changed much: the black people still live together without any money and mostly go to school together—just a few of us out on the other side of the mountain.

Mr. Austin asks people what they know about civil disobedience. Danni and Gerald talk about Nelson Mandela, Dr. King, and Rosa Parks. "All Rosa Parks wanted was to sit down," Danni says, showing off her smarts with pride. "Turns out she stood up." Danni talks to Mr. Austin, but I feel her eyes on me, like I should be *Amen*-ing. In class, like on the court, I'm fine on the side, minding my own business.

"And that spirit is still alive today." Mr. Austin walks toward his desk and clicks on the smartboard. We watch YouTube clips of the Black Lives Matter marches, but also ones about something called Occupy Wall Street and protests at high schools about standardized testing.

"I hope those students are protesting about something important," Danni says.

"Like how bad the food is in the school cafeteria," I snap, to a few laughs.

"You shouldn't complain about something that's free for you," Lex growls. I feel eyes on me, waiting for a reaction. Lex is just angry that he's here with the rest of us "regular folks" and not in AP classes like some of his friends. I wish my girl Lucy was here. She'd have cut him ear to ear with her sharp tongue, but she's in those AP classes—not Lex. I look at Gerald and Danni. Are any of us going to say something?

But we all just let it go, like we do almost every time something ignorant like that comes out of Lex's mouth. Not Jayson, though: the second Coach dropped the "thug" bomb, he stood up tall. Maybe if I started at center instead of backing up the backup, I'd stand up too. At this high school, you're only as smart as your minutes per game, batting average, or yards per carry.

Somebody—I think Ashley—mentions protesting the Vietnam War.

"The protest was not just against the killing in Vietnam, but also against young men being drafted here," Mr. Austin says.

"Drafted? What's that?" Gerald asks.

Lex and his friends create a soundtrack of sighs and stupid laughter. Mr. Austin starts to answer, but Ashley cuts him off. "Every male eighteen or older could be drafted into the military, meaning he didn't have a choice but to serve. You had to go."

"Not necessarily, Ashley," Mr. Austin corrects her, but in a gentle tone. "You could avoid the draft if you were in college, if you had connections, or if you had money."

"You mean if you were white," I whisper to Gerald. He cracks and bumps me hard.

Danni starts talking about MLK. Lex mutters something to his friends. They talk among themselves so we can't hear what they're saying, but it's not like we don't know what most of them really think.

Mr. Austin stands there like he does, his arms crossed against his chest and his glasses resting on his balding head, but showing no emotion as he waits for the class to quiet down. I've seen him do this for up to ten minutes. But Ashley just tells Lex and his friends to shut up so Austin can talk.

"One of the more famous protests against the war actually involved people your age," Mr. Austin finally says. He goes old-school, writing on the blackboard: *Tinker v. Des Moines.* "So we'll head down to the library where you'll divide into groups of two and research this court case someplace other than Wikipedia. Next week you'll present it to the class. One side will argue for Tinker, the student who protested, and the other side for the school district. And I'll pick the partners."

Gerald gives me this big, bug-eyed look since we know Austin won't let us pair up like normal. And if I pair up with Danni, Lucy's not going to be happy about that.

Austin starts reading off names, and I end up with Ashley. She's the younger sister of Dylan, our senior shooting guard who Coach almost never lets shoot, especially threes. She's smart and shoots off her mouth with the same skill that her brother shoots jumpers, except nobody applauds her talent.

"Hey, Cody," Ashley says as we walk toward the library with the rest of the class. She's small, maybe not even five feet, so my six-five frame makes me feel like a gangly giraffe.

"Hey, Ashley," I say, always so clever.

"Why do you put up with Lex's crap?" she asks, all the while scrolling on her cell. I hear she's a Twitter freak. "Lex is such a jerk."

Like with A.C. the other day on the bench, I've got no words, just a shoulder shrug.

"Like that thing he said today," Ashley says. "He assumed you get a free lunch just because—"

"But I *am* on free lunch," I say, not happy about it, but not ashamed either.

"And so are me and Dylan. You should hear the things they say about you and Danni and—"

"It isn't anything I haven't heard before." I feel bad about lying. At Inglenook, the school I attended before, people talked trash about what you did, but not about who you were. "My mom told me I'd better get used to it because that's how the world is. It's one of the reasons she moved us to Hill Top."

"Then the world's a messed-up place." Ashley never just goes with the status quo. She doesn't dress like most of the girls around here, trying to look hot. She has super-short brown hair and usually wears an oversize white T with big, black biker boots.

"Mom says it's all mind over matter," I say. "If you don't mind, then it doesn't matter." I open the library door for Ashley and she smiles.

"Dylan told me about your coach kicking Jayson off the team. He said you stepped up and stopped it from being worse. That took some courage," Ashley says.

I shrug, embarrassed. "Maybe. You didn't see the fight?" I throw two fake punches into the air. "*Bam bam*."

"Cody, I love my older brother but not enough to sit through a stupid basketball game."

We talk about nothing much else until we sit down at the computer, where she goes right to Wikipedia to look up *Tinker v. Des Moines*. That smile from earlier gets bigger as she reads about the case. I read over her shoulder about these kids who protested the Vietnam War by wearing black armbands to school.

"So who do you want to be?" I ask, passing the ball her way.

"Tinker." Like Lucy and like Jayson, Ashley enjoys the center spotlight. I'm content on the bench just belonging. For some, the game's about showing off and showing you're better than others. I'm just happy to be part of something that isn't broken. "You okay with that, Cody?"

I nod my head, but my eyes are on my phone as I text Lucy, the center of *my* attention.

MONDAY AFTER SCHOOL
DECEMBER 5
Vestavia Hills High School gym

"Call you after practice," I tell Lucy, like I do every day at this time. She answers with a kiss to my cheek. She's on tiptoe. What she lacks in size, she makes up for in spunk. She dyes her short hair red, keeps a gold locket I gave her around her neck, and like Ashley, always has her pink phone in hand. She takes a pic of us, then posts it, as if the world needs more C & L photos.

"You have to study for Austin's civics test, so don't be—" she starts, but I cut her off with a kiss of my own. No cheek, full court lip press. We get a few "get a room" catcalls from guys on the team going into the locker room. Truth is, with Lucy, I'd rather study her anatomy than civics, algebra, or whatever. "Later, Co," she whispers, and then she walks away. I watch her go, enjoying the view.

"Spend more time on ball and less on booty," Lex says. A slap to the back of my head serves as an exclamation point. He laughs. His spit falls like rain on my neck.

I head into the locker room and change into my practice uniform. I look across at Jayson's locker. Everybody has decorated their locker with stupid stuff, except Jayson, who just has a handwritten Post-It note that says "Jayson Davis #45." The locker seems lonely, as if it misses him.

As we head toward the court, Lex pushes past me. "Out of the way, Domino."

"What did he call you?" A.C. asks from two steps behind.

I watch Lex's $300 Jordans smack against the floor. "I don't want to talk about it." A.C.'s skin is dark like Gerald's, darker than Jayson's, but I'm so light that people might not even guess that my mom is black.

"He's not calling you—"

"Move, Mr. Carter!" Coach shouts at A.C. Like Jayson, A.C. transferred to the Hills from the hood. Coach, Lex, and some others made them feel as welcome as jock itch. I don't get their crap because I don't gobble up game-time minutes like A.C., Jayson, and Gerald do.

We're no sooner on the court than Coach gives us an earful about what losers we are, even though we won the game. We beat Brook because A.C. hit a three at the buzzer, which made the crowd explode in joy. But even after A.C. won the game, Coach yelled at him like he was a dog that did something wrong.

"Discipline, people, discipline," Coach starts. I think he's got a file of these court virtue speeches. We sit on the floor so we're small, while he walks in front of us, casting a shadow like a giant.

The players, except for Dylan, hang their heads like they weighed a hundred pounds, playing the solemn card. I'm biting my lip from laughing at Coach's pious pose. I see A.C. doing the same. If Jayson was here, he'd be busting a gut.

Coach breaks us up into the normal two groups, so with Jayson out, I'm in at backup center. With Lex sitting up high on the circle running the offense, everything slows to a snail's pace. Gerald feeds Lex the ball and then gets open, but Lex can't—or won't—pass it back. Coach blows the whistle and tells me to play defense against him. This is not going to be good.

"Watch me, Lex!" Coach blows the whistle again, calls for the ball, and dribbles. He turns left, but I stay square and in front. Coach head-fakes, tries another way, but I'm glue. His shoulder rams into my chest. I fall, and my back smacks against the wood with a mighty thud.

"You see, Lex, you can draw a foul if you move quick enough," Coach says.

Gerald, A.C., and Dylan help me up. "That was a charge," Dylan whispers. I nod.

"What are you gonna do, Cody?" A.C. asks as Lex walks to the foul line. I scoop up the ball, dribble down the court, and set up at the opposite foul line. Even with Coach's whistle blowing and people screaming not to do something stupid, I'm calm. I bounce the ball twice and sink the first free throw. It's free all right, like playing pick-up with Jayson; there's no real pressure to perform. I can take my mind off everything and direct it to the bouncing ball, then follow it as my second shot falls into the net.

MONDAY NIGHT
DECEMBER 5
Hill Top Apartments

"Are you suspended from school too?" I pass the ball to Jayson. It's twilight at the apartment complex where we live. Two dudes, two moms, no dads, and one dream to get out.

"Nah, I just didn't feel like showing up." Dribble. Dribble. Step. Leap. Layup.

"Lex was trash-talking you," I say. Jayson passes the ball back to me. I go to the foul line. Bounce. Bounce. Shoot. *Swish*. Here, with no coach to yell and no plays to run, everything goes in the net. "He was talking about how he took your minutes and he won't give 'em back."

"How many minutes? How many points?" Jayson asks.

"Fourteen minutes. Four points. Two rebounds."

"And no assists," Jayson adds. "Ball never leaves Lex's hands except toward the hoop."

We go back and forth trash-talking Lex until my phone rings. "Fight the Power"—an old song Lucy loves—is my ringtone for her. She picked it out. I didn't disagree. "What's up?" I ask. Jayson dribbles, dunks. It's what he does.

Lucy goes on about studying for Mr. Austin's civics test. She doesn't need to study, I do—but she holds back from saying that. Usually, she's got a big mouth, which I like. Sometimes it gets her in trouble with some teachers, but not Austin. I hear Austin's AP class is hard, but he's soft on Lucy because he sponsors the debate team where Lucy and Ashley shine, like Jayson shines on the court. Maybe I'm not the best at anything, but I'm plugged into the power. I listen to Lucy for a while, which is something I never tire of, until I end with, "Later, Luce."

I bury the phone in my jeans. Jayson's throwing up shots that miss to practice rebounding.

"Jayson, can I ask you something?" He moves toward me, dribbling all the way. I point at the numbers on his sweaty, blue practice jersey that he must have worn home after Coach kicked him off the team. "How come you wear number 45?"

"Coach doesn't like it," he says. "He has rules that centers wear certain numbers, but I told him I wanted 45. We had our first stare-down over it, and I'm not sure why, but he let me have it. And that's the last time Coach ever listened to what I had to say."

Jayson's the best player on the team, but Coach treats him like he's the worst. "So, 45?"

"Everybody back in the hood is always bragging about their 45s."

I nod. Like Jayson, I grew up in Birmingham, but I left there in junior high.

"So, I never wanted that life," Jayson continued. "I decided that the first time I got a uniform, I'd want number 45 to remind me that if I don't play hard and study, I won't get a college scholarship and I'll be back in the hood."

Jayson's so focused on basketball most of the time, most people wouldn't guess that basketball's not his end goal. He's got dreams beyond the court too.

"So what's Coach's deal with you?" I ask. Jayson bounces the ball hard against the pitted pavement. "I wonder if it's because you're a transfer student. Maybe because you took Lex's minutes." The ball bouncing sounds like a gunshot. "Or maybe it's because you're black."

The ball stays in Jayson's hand. "You think?" he fires back.

"Coach doesn't like it," I say, "but he plays you, A.C., and Gerald."

"The way he coaches, limiting our freedom, I wonder why. Who does this old, angry guy with no game think he is, telling me how to do it? What gives him the right? Because he's old?" Jayson hands me the ball.

"Or wait, maybe it's because he's white."

"You think?" Jayson cracks again. I drop the ball from laughing too hard.

"You gonna get some minutes now?" Jayson asks. I shrug. "Cody, out here you got game, but you get all caught up in the coach's bull, trying to do it his way. Shoot, don't pass."

"That's not my job," I remind Jayson, who can shoot and pass and rebound.

"Then what *is* your job?"

I motion for Jayson to run toward the hoop and toss him a perfect alley-oop that he slams home for two points. There is the answer: making others look good.

THURSDAY AFTER SCHOOL
DECEMBER 8
Vestavia Hills High School gym

"Pass, don't shoot!" Coach yells at A.C. for the forty-fifth time, though that's just a guess. We've lost—gotten crushed actually—our two games without Jayson. It seems Coach wants to take it out on the players putting points on the board. He gives A.C. and Gerald extra attention, but not in a good way. Me he doesn't bother. Dylan's getting grief instead of me. Thanks for taking the bullet.

A.C. passes to Lex, who gathers it in, fakes left, turns right. Shoots. Misses. Yawn.

"Why don't you let me shoot?" A.C. says too loudly. "Least I can hit the net."

"I'm the coach," Coach yells, pointing to the windbreaker he's wearing that says COACH in all caps. A.C. is shaking his head like he's got water in his ear or something.

"If you don't like it, then . . ." Coach says nothing else, leaving that "then" out there like a piñata. A.C. swings.

"No, I don't like it. Back at North, I always got to—"

"This isn't North. This is Vestavia Hills, and I'm the coach. You do things my way."

"Your way ain't working." A.C. bounces the ball hard, almost to cover the words.

"*Isn't*, not *ain't*." Coach crosses his arms. "You want to get suspended like your cuz?"

"Cuz? For serious?" A.C. clutches the ball in both hands like he's trying to crush it. Just like the other day, I know that's my cue. I stand up, step in front of Coach, and block the hard throw A.C. hurtles toward

Coach's head. I bear the brunt of the blow in my chest.

Nobody says anything for a few seconds, then Coach blows his whistle and we're back to the scrimmage. A.C. stays on the floor, but his shot and his spirit have left him.

When I come onto the court for my token practice minutes, Lex gets in my face since I'm playing center against him. "I thought you were smart like that girlfriend of yours," Lex says.

I say nothing.

"If A.C. sits, then you might get some minutes. Stupid," Lex says.

More nothing from me, but Lex is all dog to my bone. "Good luck, Domino!"

I play a few minutes. One assist, no fouls, no rebounds. Just good team defense.

After practice, A.C. finds me. "Thanks, Cody." Fist bump. All good. "Can I ask you something?"

I nod my answer and use my practice jersey to wipe the little bit of sweat from my face.

"Why do you let Lex call you that name?" he asks. "He's disrespecting you and—"

"Like Coach did when he called you cuz?" I ask, and A.C. just shrugs his broad shoulders.

"What are we gonna do?" I stare at my worn blue Chucks, then glare over at Lex's Jordans. He uses them not only to drudge down the court but to walk on water, untouched.

A.C. grunts in reply. I pick up a loose ball and dribble as we walk to the locker room. I see Lex and Coach staring at me. I start thinking about how much I think about stuff. I stand at the free throw line. Bounce. Bounce. Shoot. Miss. Lex laughs hard.

"Shake it off," A.C. says. "It doesn't matter if you miss in practice, just in the game."

"I have to *get* in the game," I remind him. A.C. picks up the ball, cuts to the basket, and motions for me to pass like Jayson taught me. The sphere lands in his hands as he soars through the air. The dunk rattles the basket.

"Some people score," A.C. declares like gospel. "And some people pass."

I think about Mr. Austin's class and about how some people lead while other people follow.

"Hey, Cody, the benches need polishing,"

Lex yells from across the gym. "Guess you'll do that next game." Some of his friends laugh, and then they all head toward the locker room.

I look at the folded-up bleachers, imagine them pulled out and everybody standing up. Game's on the line, but my butt's not on the bench. I close my eyes and imagine the scene: standing at the free throw line, noise all around me, but at the center there's nothing but calm because I know in my mind that none of it really matters. It's just two points in a world that's full of big challenges, and deep down, I know I'm up to them. Bounce. Bounce. Shoot. *Swish.*

MONDAY MORNING
DECEMBER 12
Vestavia Hills High School

"You have to have rules in a school so everybody can get an education," I mumble, staring at the smartboard. Ashley went PowerPoint crazy. "And the students who wore armbands to protest the war disrupted the school, so . . . so. . . ."

"So?" Mr. Austin prods me. Ashley clears her throat as she watches me choke. I don't like talking in class, especially up in front.

"So, what? A war where people are dying is more important than stupid rules," she starts, and even though it's supposed to be a debate between us, I let her do most of the talking as she explains how even students have free speech. She even quotes the Supreme Court opinion: "Students do not lose their constitutional rights at the schoolhouse door."

Mr. Austin interrupts her to let me speak, but I have nothing to say. It's silly arguing about something that happened fifty years ago at a school in Iowa when we have real problems in Alabama now.

"In conclusion, let me quote Edmund Burke, whoever that is," Ashley says, then laughs. Not something she does a whole lot, I noticed while we worked on the project. She is one serious student. "'The only thing necessary for the triumph of evil is for good men to do nothing.'"

"Or as that other great philosopher, John Lennon, said in the seventies, 'Power to the people, right on!'" Mr. Austin adds. He thanks us, and we head back to our desks.

"Good job, Cody," Ashley says.

"You too." I'm not used to anybody telling me that. I almost think she's busting me.

"I mean what I said," Ashley says as she sits down near the front. "And what that Burke guy said too. If you don't say or do anything, then bad stuff's gonna keep happening, right?"

"Maybe," I shrug in utter confusion. Even as Danni and Whitney debate, I'm tuned out, thinking about what Ashley said. If I am a good man, then what's the right thing to do?

• • •

That quote from that Burke guy is still on my mind when I grab a seat next to Jayson at lunch. He's got a pile of fries and a pool of ketchup.

"Jayson, do you get to practice tonight?" A.C. asks.

Jayson says something through a mouthful of food that we take as a yes.

"So what are you going to do differently?" I ask him. "I mean with Coach."

Jayson mocks a boxer throwing right jabs. A.C. and Gerald crack up at this, but not me.

"What's your problem, Cody?" A.C. gives me a hard stare.

I tell them about the project in civics and the quote that Ashley found, but they don't seem interested in what I've got to say. Instead, Jayson's going on about getting in Coach's face.

"Dom, are you crazy?" I ask him. Now Jayson's got me in the hard-stare crosshairs too.

"What are you saying?" Two big fries drowned in ketchup disappear into his mouth.

"Einstein said the definition of crazy was doing the same things but expecting different results. So next time Coach gets up in your face about something, what are you going to do?"

Even though the cafeteria is crazy-loud, it is almost like somebody muted our table. Everybody's looking at Jayson. We're going one-on-one, but we're not in his court.

"Well?"

"Maybe I'll remind him that without me, he's got no team," Jayson answers.

"Thanks a lot, Jayson!" A.C. and Gerald say at the same time.

"That's not what I mean." Jayson offers

fist-bump apologies. "I came to the school
to be safe and play ball, that's it. I won't let
anything get in my way," Jayson says. He stuffs
the last handful of fries into his mouth. But
Jayson's words aren't going to be enough, I
think. When they go one-on-one, Coach wins
because he controls the net, the ball, the court.
We live in his world.

Jayson stands, tosses his garbage. He's not
somebody I want as an enemy. I make sure
we're good before I go. "All good, Cody," he
says, but I wonder if he's right. Am I all good?

TUESDAY AFTER SCHOOL
DECEMBER 13
Vestavia Hills High School gym

"Great game last night," I whisper to Jayson before we start Coach's silent stretching exercises. First-teamers normally go up front, but Jayson, Gerald, and A.C. hang with me in back.

Jayson nods, starts stretching, but starts talking too. "I didn't get all my minutes." With Jayson starting last night, we had the game by the end of the first half. Coach pulled him for

Lex. I bet Coach wanted to grind Jayson down. Jayson spent the last minutes of the game joining me as a pine jockey.

"No talking during stretching exercises!" Coach yells our way. I bite my bottom lip.

Jayson looks over at me. No winks this time, just a hard stare. "I can't do this, Cody."

"Does somebody not understand my English? No talking during my exercises."

"You were right, Cody, this is crazy." Jayson's volume goes up a notch.

"Do I need to use smaller words?" Coach glares bullet holes in Jayson's chest.

"The people on TV talk when they do their exercises," Jayson says, just loud enough.

A.C. cracks up.

Coach blows his whistle and moves like a bulldozer toward us. "Bleachers. Up and down, ten times." He blows the whistle again. A.C. takes off like a sprinter.

Jayson stands in place, big hands on powerful hips, not moving a single hard muscle.

"I'm sick of your attitude." Coach is back in Jayson's face. "I let you—"

"And I'm sick of your crap," Jayson returns fire. "Attitudes don't win games. Coaches don't win games. Skills like mine win games, so get out of my face and let me play my—"

"Give me your uniform." Coach reaches out his right hand. I see it's shaking slightly, but Jayson is icy like January. In fact, he's breaking out a rare smile. The smile disappears only for a second when he lifts practice number 45 over his head. Jayson places the jersey softly into Coach's hand like he's putting his head on a pillow.

"If you want his uniform, you can have mine too." Gerald rips off his jersey and hurls it.

The two stand in front of Coach: a wall of iron muscle and stronger will. I look up at A.C., who retreats from the bleachers. Lex and his buds are laughing it up like this minor mutiny is some comedy. The scene reminds me more of one of those action movies where everybody's got guns pointed and you wonder who will fire first. I wish I was like Lucy, always with phone in hand, because this would make a great vid. Hashtag showdown at the not-OK Corral.

"That wasn't ten times up and down," Coach barks at A.C.

"I know how to count." A.C. pulls the jersey over his head, uses it to wipe away his sweat, and then tosses it at Coach's feet. "And I also calculate that you've lost sixty percent of your starters."

Coach starts to blow his whistle, but Jayson, Gerald, and A.C. turn their backs to Coach and walk toward the locker room, wearing no shirts, but a thick skin of self-respect.

● ● ●

"Dang, Co, that's a story," Lucy says after I tell her what happened at practice. I'm at her house, which is like four times bigger than my crib. We study at the dining room table. Her mom's just in the next room, pretending to load the dishwasher, but she's really listening in and playing guard.

"I should've done something." But, like I do in games, I choked.

"He wasn't picking on you." She pushes

her chair a little closer. Lucy smells sweet, like when Mom opens up a women's magazine full of perfume samples. "It isn't your fight, Co."

I point at the civics book in front of me, leaf through it until I find the section on the civil rights movement, then find a pic of the Selma march. "That doesn't mean I can't take a stand."

"But you *love* being on that team," she says. "Not as much as you love *me*, but almost."

I blush, but before I speak, she's looking at her phone, not me. She scrolls, reads, and texts.

"I'm gonna tell everybody," Lucy says when she pauses the tap-tap-tap.

"That you love me?"

She laughs, almost snorts. "No, about what happened at practice."

"No, don't do that," I say. "It'll get back to me and I'll get in trouble."

"Everybody's gotta get in trouble every now and then." Lucy points at the civics book. Even though she's Miss Debate-Club-and-Student-Council, I've seen her risk getting in trouble in order to stand up if something's not fair. "How do you think revolutions start? Somebody's gotta stand front and center and say no."

I start to tell Lucy about what Ashley said, but her pretty browns seem to be turning jealous green, so I simply say, "Maybe." Unlike my buds who get their minutes, it's not like I have anything to lose.

I inch closer, take my hands off the book, and put one hand on Lucy's back, but she's not having it. I shrug.

She turns back to her phone, while I page through the civics book. March on Washington. Selma. Vietnam War protests. Seems like everybody in the sixties, like Austin said, spent their time on the streets. They definitely weren't watching YouTube.

"It's late, Mr. Hopkins," Lucy's mom says. She always calls me mister, like I'm a grown man instead of sixteen and a half.

"I know."

I stand to leave, give Lucy a Mom-approved kiss on the cheek, and walk toward the door, not feeling anything like a mister or a man.

"Good luck on your test tomorrow, Mr. Hopkins."

Never mind the civics test. I'm about to find out whether I'm a good man who stands up or a bystander who just stays seated.

WEDNESDAY AFTERNOON
DECEMBER 14
Vestavia Hills High School gym

During lunch, Principal Page comes to our table and tells A.C. and Gerald to come with him to his office. Not me, not Jayson. We just sit like two losers not picked for a team. It's only when I go into the locker room for practice that I see the two of them suiting up in practice jerseys.

"What happened?" I ask. They talk over each other, but the gist is that Principal Page said if they apologized to Coach, he'd let them back on the team. They said they didn't like it, but it was a small price to pay for getting to play. They said Coach must've been told to cool it because he didn't look them in the eye as he mumbled an apology too. "What about Jayson?" I ask.

They avoid looking at each other or me. The locker room floor beneath them grabs their attention like some wreck on the freeway until finally A.C. says, "No, he's off the team for good. What he did was stupid. I don't see that our leaving the team would help him, and it just hurts us."

"That's not what you thought yesterday," I snap. I don't know why I'm mad at them because it's not like *I* did anything either, but something about this seems wrong. "I thought you—"

"We didn't think," A.C. says. "Besides, I think everything is gonna be OK."

I picture Coach and how he stares at my buds from stretching exercises to scrimmage, like he's waiting for them to fail so he can rage at them. *It's not gonna be OK*, I think.

During scrimmage, I'm in for Jayson—
shoes so big to fill that I feel small, like a
child's toy. And I must be made of wood, the
way Lex hacks at me with his lumberjack
hands on almost every play, which goes to
show how stupid he is. It's not like I'm going
to take the shot, since Coach's offense hinges
on the center distributing the ball, not taking
it to the hoop.

When I get to the foul line, Lex
accidentally-on-purpose bumps into me.
"Good luck, Domino," he whispers. I bounce
the ball too hard and too often, focusing not
on the hoop but on Lex and Coach's hollers
and all the nonsense.

"Shoot already!" Lex shouts.

The ball clangs off the backboard as I miss
the first. Lex passes it back to me, hard, like
he's trying to hurt me or something. I step
away from the line and take a deep breath. I
avoid the eyes of Lex and Coach willing me
to fail. Instead, I concentrate on the school
banner hanging up in the rafters. The Rebels.
We had a mutiny, but now we need a rebellion.

Coach yells at me to return to the foul line, but I push away the distractions. It's a free throw, and I let my mind be just that: free. Bounce. Bounce. Shoot. The ball goes in. One point. But I don't stop there. One point leads to another to another. Every winning game starts with a single shot going in.

"Cody, bleachers, now!" Coach punishes me for my defiance. I take it as a badge. Just before I hit the first step, A.C. and Gerald congratulate me on hitting my free throws.

"If we had a DH like in baseball," A.C. says, "we'd get you at the foul line all the time."

"I'd need to get my minute to get my chance."

"Bleachers!" Coach yells at me again. It's time. One step, one shot, one woman standing up on a bus, other people sitting down at a lunch counter. Back in the day, a revolution started with somebody firing the first bullet. But I don't need a gun, fist, or knife to do that. The best weapons now, it seems to me, are a phone and a hashtag.

• • •

"Cody?" Ashley asks. I guess I spoke with her enough during our assignment that she knows the sound of my voice, not that she probably ever expected to hear it over her phone.

"I need a favor." I hate saying those words.

She's silent, but there's nothing but noise behind me as I stand outside my building near the gray court listening to a soundtrack of slams. Jayson's taking his anger out on the backboard.

"You know that thing you said about how evil wins when good people do nothing?"

"Well, somebody else said it. I just shared it." She laughs. "Kind of like retweeting."

"I'm a boy, not a bird, so I don't tweet." Ashley laughs again. I like the sound of it.

"So, does Lucy know you're talking to me?" Ashley asks. Behind me booms the loud thud of dunks. "I mean, I don't want any trouble with her."

"No, but I'll tell her," I confess. "Guess what? *I* want trouble from her even less."

She laughs again. Who knew I was this funny? "So what do you need, Cody?"

"A hashtag," I say with all seriousness in my

voice. I proceed to explain my ignorance of all the stuff that seems to suck up everybody else's time. "So can you help me, Ashley?"

"What's it for?"

I tell her about what went down with Coach. She goes all silent again. "Ashley?"

"Look, I'll help you one time, get it started, but that's it," she explains. "This isn't my battle to fight. It's yours. So what do you want to do? Fire the coach? What do we call it?"

In the background, I hear Jayson crash another dunk. "Bring back 45."

9

THURSDAY MORNING
DECEMBER 15
Vestavia Hills High School

"Have you seen it?" A.C. shoves his phone in my face.

"Seen what?" I act like I have no idea what he's talking about, even though I can feel the phone in my pocket blowing up. I'm casual as I peer at the posts that Ashley talked me through creating. #BringBack45.

"Look, it's on Tumblr, Instagram, everywhere. Viral!"

I pretend my nose itches and scratch it to hide my yawn. Spreading the news everywhere took until four in the morning.

Pretty soon some other friends come up, talking about the same thing. All of them follow and then retweet the latest anonymous post about how Coach treats black players and about the racist remarks he's made.

"Think Jayson did it?" A.C. asks no one in particular.

"I doubt it," I say. Jayson's hands are not half skin, half phone like Lucy's and Ashley's. "But Coach is gonna think he did it anyway."

"Like Austin said the other day in class," Gerald says, "power to the people, right on!"

The bell rings for first hour, sending conversations and bodies in different directions toward class. Everybody but me. I'm on my way to the bathroom. I close the little stall door, take out my phone, and share my bile with the whole world by posting more anonymous stuff about Coach.

Just after I get to first hour late, Mr. Austin even mentions the hashtag in class. For the first time, I feel like a big shot, even if nobody except Ashley knows it's me. I guess there are two people who might suspect me: Lucy and Coach. With Lucy, I'll tell her as soon I see her. With Coach, I'll know whether he suspects me as soon as he sees me. He'll have my uniform and my head, I'm just not sure in which order.

• • •

"Whoever did this is gutless!" Coach shouts. The only thing we've stretched at practice so far is our patience as Coach goes on and on about what he calls "that tweet nonsense."

"The essence of any sport is respect," Coach starts. He finally moves off the "tweet nonsense" rant and onto one of his canned speeches about the virtues of a successful athlete. He doesn't mention bullying, his stock-in-trade, as one of these virtues.

We get through stretching and exercises with a minimum of screaming. I wonder if Page told Coach he needed to turn down the volume. I smile. Maybe "that tweet nonsense" is already working.

The scrimmage starts. I'm on the bench, but the real game is the social media offensive happening outside this gym. About halfway through, I get on the court as the first team comes down with the ball. Dylan takes a jumper that clangs off the rim almost as loud as Coach yelling "No!" at him. The ball shoots out and I haul it in, dribble twice, make the long pass, but then cut toward the basket for the give-and-go. When the ball comes back to me, Lex has thundered down the court. He's not in position, so I cut toward the basket. Our uniforms barely touch, but he crashes to the court. I plant my foot, leap as high as I can, and lay the ball against the backboard. It drops for two.

Coach blows the whistle. It doesn't just stop the play—it seems to stop time. Everybody's eyes dart back and forth between me, Lex, and Coach until Coach calls it his way. "Charging foul."

I hear A.C., Gerald, and Dylan curse under their breath. I offer my hand to Lex, but he ignores it. The starters take the ball down the court. I get into position but ease off so Lex gets the pass. He's at the top of the key, ball in hand, like a marble statue. I tuck in my left shoulder as if I was a blocking tackle rather than a backup center and smash as hard as I can into Lex.

"Now *that's* a charging foul!" I shout. Lex crashes, Coach whistles, I smile. My triple-double. I glance up at the banner of the Rebels, and for the first time, I feel I've earned that name.

10

THURSDAY EVENING
DECEMBER 15
Lucy Grafton's house

"So, are you proud of me?" I ask Lucy after telling her I'm behind #BringBack45. I don't tell her about Coach kicking me out of practice or Lex threatening to kick my butt.

"I thought you didn't want to get in trouble," she says, kind of pouty, which makes her look extra cute. "I thought you said it wasn't your fight. I thought—"

"And I thought you said that making

trouble is how revolutions start," I remind her.
"I didn't get you involved, because I didn't want
to get *you* into trouble. You've got stuff going
for you, and you'd hate me if you got kicked off
of the debate team or something. I thought—"

Lucy kisses me slow and soft since her
mom's out doing something in the garage.
When we hear the door open, we break it up.
"You think it's gonna make a difference?"
she asks.

"Maybe *doing* something makes a difference."

"I want to help. No, Co, I don't *want* to
help. I *need* to help."

"No, Lucy. This is my battle now. You
don't need—"

"Co, there's no *my*, there's just *ours* and *we*.
What should we do?"

I turn over my phone, bring it up, and see
that the number of followers has more than
doubled just since after school. The idea kicks
like a donkey. "We should break up."

"What? No! Why?" The panic in her voice
almost distracts me from the tears in her eyes.

"We break up and you tell everybody

it's because I thought the #BringBack45 was stupid, and you be the public face of it. I'll post stuff, but nobody can know it's me until it's over. Coach would kick me off the team, and guys like Lex would kick my—"

"You can't get kicked off the team—the team you love almost as much as you love me," Lucy reminds me. The tips of my ears tingle and burn. "When will it be over?"

I kiss her for the last time in who knows how long. "When we win."

11

FRIDAY EVENING
DECEMBER 16
Vestavia Hills High School gym

Friday started with Lucy and me having a
for-public-consumption break-up fight and
moved next into the rumor that Jayson's mom
is trying to get him into another school so
he can play. Now the day is ending with us
getting pounded by the Hueytown team. Even
though Coach keeps saying we'll come back
and win, nobody believes it, especially when he
already put me in for the last two minutes of

the half. He might as well have waved a white flag. I blew my chance to shine: nothing on the score sheet except for zeros and two fouls. And there's a lot fewer people, especially students, in the stands than usual.

During halftime, the guy who has been Coach Cool for the past couple days melts down. All eyes are on Coach, so nobody even sees me take my cell out. I hide it under my crossed arms. I'll get the video up on #BringBack45 before the half starts. It's a rant-fest for the ages, filled with quotable moments. My favorite is when he yells at A.C. for already having three fouls, then says, "It's basketball, not guerrilla warfare" and starts making ape sounds. Coach ends with "You all stink! Stop acting like losers," then says, "Now, go play with confidence." He's Mr. Mixed-Messages for sure.

I hang back as the rest of the team jogs out of the locker room. "Let's go, Cody!" he yells at me. Since I touched the ball, I've earned his wrath.

"Coach, I think I twisted my ankle. I just need a minute." His eyelids flicker, and his mouth twitches like he's got a smart comeback ready to burst out like an alien from his chest.

"Walk it off." That's his answer for every injury. Broken arm? Walk it off. Gunshot wound? Walk it off. Amputated feet? Stump it off, I guess. Coach turns his back and heads off toward the gym. I upload the video, fist-bump Jayson's empty locker, and put away my phone.

As I fake-hobble toward the gym, it's like they started the game already because there's a ton of noise. It's the loudest it's been since we scored the first of ten pathetic baskets. When I reach the gym, I identify the source of the noise and smile wide. Up in the bleachers, which are now packed with students, stand Lucy and Ashley. Together they hold a huge white blanket with "#BringBack45" painted on it in black. Around them stand maybe fifty students: some white kids I recognize, along with all the black kids at school.

The chant "Bring Back 45" starts with Lucy, and pretty soon other people, mostly students, join in. Coach's face turns a deep shade of red.

All the players on both teams are standing, pointing at people, and talking to one another. The coach on the other team looks confused— he's gotta get a Twitter account.

"Sit down!" Coach yells at us. In the bleachers, everybody keeps chanting, although they've changed it up. They shout "bring back," then clap twice, and when they say "forty," they hold up four fingers on their right hand, then on "five," they hold up five fingers on their right hand. The only person who looks more upset than Coach is Brittany Holland, Vestavia Hills cheerleading captain, since this chant is getting more response than anything she ever led.

The refs motion—because they can't shout over the noise—for the coaches to meet at center court. They huddle up like it's football season. The chant's still going strong, but it dies down when almost everybody reaches for a phone at the same time. My guess is they're all looking at my video of Coach's half-time meltdown. The noise rises like the tide.

I know I'm right when, instead of chanting,

people start mocking that gorilla sound from the vid. All the players on the bench, with the exception of Lex and his friends, are cracking up. The refs yell at Coach to get his team onto the court, which he does. But everybody in the stands and in the school knows there's no sense in doing that. The real contest isn't the one on the basketball court between the Vestavia Hills Rebels and the Hueytown High Gophers. It's the one in the court of public opinion between an old-school coach and the new media of "#BringBack45."

12

"So this is it?" I shout at Jayson as I launch up an alley-oop pass. He leaps, catches the ball, palms it in his right hand, and slams it into the net. "You're the enemy now."

Jayson passes the ball back to me. "I need to play. It's the only way out."

"Are they gonna let you wear number 45 at your new school?"

Jayson's wide smile is his answer. He motions

for me to run the play again. "I think Hoover is on our schedule pretty soon, not that I pay attention since I don't play."

I dribble and pass. He dunks and scores. "You got no confidence in your game, so you got no game," Jayson tells me. "Out here, every pass is perfect, and most every shot goes in. So why not at practice?"

"I don't know. Except at the foul line, I choke. I let people down."

Jayson laughs, but in a friendly tone. "You didn't let *me* down." He hadn't believed for one second that I really broke up with Lucy or that I had nothing to do with #BringBack45.

"But it didn't work," I sigh.

"Not yet, but I didn't get this good overnight." He hits a long three to prove his point. "From the thing on Friday, it seems you got some support, but what you need is teammates."

"Sure, Dom, I'll ask Lex." Jayson snorts at the idea of it.

I think about the guys on the team. One by one, their faces flash in front of me. I wonder if they understand this isn't just about race, but about power and control. Probably no white guy on the team suffers more than Dylan, a shooting guard Coach won't let shoot.

"But you can tell all the guys that when I play against you, any of you get in my lane, I'll knock you down." Jayson laughs again. Maybe his new coach will understand that more than anything, even minutes, Jayson wants respect.

• • •

"Cody, what up?" Dylan asks once he gets over the surprise of hearing my voice.

"I wanted to ask you something," I say slowly. Other than talking at practice, I can't recall any conversation I've ever had with Dylan in person or on the phone.

"If it's about my sister Ashley, I don't— "

My face flushes. "No."

"I heard you and Lucy broke up, so I thought you thought—"

"No." Harder this time, with the fury of a blocked shot.

"So to what do I owe the honor of this call?" Dylan asks in a joking tone.

I hem and haw, talk about Jayson, Coach, and the team in general, until he cuts me off. "Look, Cody, if you think I'm going to jeopardize my spot for Jayson, it ain't happening."

"Jayson's not coming back. That's why that whole #BringBack45 thing is stupid."

Dylan laughs. "I dare you to say that tomorrow to my face, because I don't believe you."

"It's true."

Dylan says nothing, so I'm thinking maybe he's hung up. "Dylan, you there?"

"Cody, say what you gotta say, but don't lie to me, not if you want my help," Dylan snaps. "The video from Coach's half-time speech means it had to be somebody on the team. I don't think A.C. or Gerald would risk it. But don't worry, I'll keep it a secret."

I ball up my left fist and bang it hard into my leg. Secrets in high school are like sharks in the water: they always come up, and sometimes they bite your head off.

I ramble on more about the bigger point,

ending with, "So it's not about Jayson anymore. It's about Coach trying to control all of us, not to make us winners but just to show he can. I don't know about you, Dylan, but I love basketball, and he's sucking all the fun out of it."

A pause. "So, what do you want, Cody?" I wish we were having this talk in person so I could see the expression on Dylan's face, because all I sense in his voice is impatience and anger.

"Be a teammate for the greater good," I say. "Stand up for—"

Dylan talks over me. "Okay, I got another question for you."

"What?"

"What took you so long to ask?" Dylan inquires. I relax my left hand and thrust it out in front of me, an air fist bump to a teammate miles away who just grew a lot closer. Maybe there's some room on that Birmingham chessboard for black and white to move together.

13

MONDAY AFTERNOON
DECEMBER 19
Vestavia Hills High School

"'You ever heard of free speech?'—that's what I asked them." It's lunchtime, and I'm hiding behind the school talking on my phone to Lucy, who is curled up in the back of her car. She's just told me that the second she walked into school this morning, she was greeted not at all happily by Principal Page and Coach. I want to hear her story, but I want even more to see her. Whose idea was this fake breakup?

"So they talked about me causing a disruption and somebody could've gotten hurt, but the way I see it is, the only thing that got hurt was Coach's feelings. Well, big deal."

"It's probably over for me today," I whisper. "He's got to know I did it."

She laughs, and I miss her more. "Your coach is not the sharpest knife in the drawer."

"It's up to two thousand followers, thanks to the video of Coach and some videos people took of you leading the chant."

"I hope they got my good side," Lucy says, laughing. I want to shrink down into this phone and text myself to her.

"So, what did you do yesterday?" Lucy asks. It had been a rare day because we didn't talk, and it felt like a day without breathing.

"I helped Jayson pack his stuff. He and his mom are moving to Hoover. She found a school that said he's eligible according to how they read the rules. I doubt that he'd have come back anyway."

"So all this for nothing?"

"Not nothing. If Coach gets fired, that's

something, or even if people get together and talk about things at school. If Jayson would've been white, then—"

She finishes, "None of this would have happened." And we enjoy the thought in silence for a second.

"So what did *you* do Sunday?" I ask.

"A little something called a surprise, Co." She's in full whisper mode.

"What does that mean?"

"See you at the assembly. Your friend Ashley is going to help me."

Oh, right, I remember. An email had gone out to parents that Page had called an assembly about the protest. I had heard about it not from my mom but from A.C.

"You're not going to do the chant or banner again?" I ask, smiling ear to ear.

"I think it's free speech, but Page told me if it happened again, he wouldn't put me on in-school suspension—he'd kick me out of school. And you know my mom wouldn't love that."

"She'd love that about as much as she loves *me*."

Lucy goes silent. I close my eyes, picture her face smiling and reaching out to meet mine. The silence breaks as the bell rings to end second lunch. "See you later, Co," she whispers.

"I hope to see more of you soon, L.," I whisper right back. In a matter of seconds, she sends me a selfie of her kissing the screen. I put my lips on my phone and walk on air into school. I'm like the solar system with all the planets in my life spinning around a sun at the center: Lucy.

14

TUESDAY MORNING
DECEMBER 20
Vestavia Hills High School gym

Principal Page stands behind the microphone.
It somehow makes him look huge. I'm sitting
as far away from Lucy as I can be, which helps
maintain the illusion. Behind Page stand
Coach, Lex's dad, other big-neck Boosters, and
two school board guys in gray suits. Behind
them are two men in blue suits: Vestavia Hills
Police Department. As Page moves toward the
microphone, I see Lucy whisper something

to Ashley. I see they have stuffed book bags resting against their legs. I get a bad feeling: I want to reach out and stop her from whatever she's gonna do.

"Students, I've called this assembly today," Principal Page begins, and as with most of what he says, I don't care much. I'm far enough away from Mr. Austin that I can sneak peeks at my rising number of followers. But pretty soon, I see other numbers—well, just one number: 45. Lucy, Ashley, and about a dozen other students throw into the crowd black armbands with white letters that say #BringBack45. It's pretty chaotic as people reach for them. Most of the teachers seem to be freaking out, trying to gain control, but not Mr. Austin. He sits looking like he always does, except he's got a #BringBack45 band on each arm as *Tinker v. Des Moines* comes to life again.

"I need order in this room now!" Page yells, but no one listens. It's not just the commotion of people reaching for the armbands, but there are also some people, like Lex, who are not on board. I watch as Lex rips one of the armbands off a skinny kid next to him.

Page starts again. "Students, I'm disappointed in you, and—"

"And we're disappointed in you!" Lucy shouts. Her response gets half cheers, half boos. Page snaps his fingers and the two blue suits start toward the bleachers. As they push through the crowd, some people clear out of their way, but others, all wearing #BringBack45 bands, try to block them. Mr. Austin stands in front of Lucy, but it does no good. The two men push him aside, grab Lucy's hands, and pull them behind her back. When she tries to push back, one of the cops grabs her hard around the neck. I see her locket get ripped off and fall down to the bleachers, maybe under them. People scream at the cops. To those of us from the city, the scene's too familiar, and I know telling the story with words won't get through to the people who don't want to hear it. I grab my phone and join others in filming Lucy's arrest. I tweet out the vid, send a link to the newspaper website Al.com, and contact the TV station with "Eyewitness News," which Mom watches.

"Students, we are here to learn. The incidents of . . ." and Page is off again, but most people are not listening. Instead, everybody wearing an armband follows behind the cops dragging Lucy out of the gym. I stand up to join them but stop when Page yells, "Anyone who leaves the gym will be suspended." I watch students file out of the gym, and the commotion gradually quiets. I wonder how they're gonna find a room big enough to hold ISS for one hundred kids.

After Page is done, Coach speaks. He talks a lot but doesn't say the words people want to hear. There's no "I'm sorry" or "Jayson's back on the team." Next come the Boosters, and who even cares. The message is all the same: Teachers are here to teach, students are here to learn, and all of these other issues just distract from that. Keep your eye on the ball.

After the assembly I decide to walk by the front door to see if Lucy is sitting in a squad car or what. The car's still there, but it's parked at an angle, so I can't see inside. What I can see clearly is a big white van with an antenna that says "Eyewitness News." There's a reporter and a guy with a camera filming the students who surround the police car. It's chaotic, and I see Dylan and A.C. hoist Ashley up on their broad shoulders. Gerald does the same with his girlfriend, Danni. They're both small, but they're giving everybody voice as they chant "Bring Back 45" so loud that I bet Jayson can hear it miles away in Hoover. I keep filming and uploading video. There's not a drop of rain in the sky, but I caused this tweet tsunami. I've found myself in a place I thought I'd never want to be: at the center of the storm.

15

TUESDAY AFTER SCHOOL
DECEMBER 20
Vestavia Hills High School gym

I'm late getting into the locker room to change clothes. I spent too much time searching like some prospector for Lucy's locket. Everybody else but Lex is dressed and practicing. I hope he's sick.

"Your girlfriend is whack." It's the least offensive thing Lex says when he comes up from nowhere, grabs me by the shirt, and drags me to the back of the locker room.

"You need to tell that crazy a—"

"We broke up," I lie.

"Good thing, because I heard—" and then I don't want to listen to another vile word. I try to push past him, but he jams a knee into my groin. "And that video of Coach. That was you."

"What video?" I ask. He answers with another knee, which makes me drop to mine.

"This is all garbage," Lex says. "All for stupid Jayson. Anybody who plays high school ball should have to take an intelligence test. We can get the dumb ones off the court, then those of us who are going to college instead of prison can get the minutes we need to show our stuff."

These are the most words Lex has spoken to me in his life. He just keeps putting down Jayson, and then he moves to A.C. and Gerald, for whom his words are no warmer. "They come into our nice school bringing that ghetto garbage and playground ball. We don't want it here."

I'm breathing heavy, pain still pulsing

through my body, so it's hard to focus. Not that I'm concentrating on Lex's hateful words, but on those water-walking Jordans he wears, just inches from my face. I open my mouth, jam two fingers in deep, and empty the contents of my free-lunch stomach onto Lex's expensive shoes. Once again, I'm gutless, but I couldn't be any happier.

• • •

We both get to practice a little late, him trying to clean those shoes before giving up and throwing them away, and me learning how to walk upright again. The only thing that makes me feel a little better is getting a text from Tina, one of Ashley's friends, that there's a story on the "Eyewitness News" site about a "massive protest at Vestavia Hills High School." They even linked it to #BringBack45.

When Lex and I arrive at practice around the same time, Coach makes us run the bleachers. Every step shoots pain through my body like bolts of lightning.

Normally, I could distract myself with

what's going on down on the court, except
it's stone silent and it's easy to see why:
every player, except me and Lex, wears
#BringBack45 armbands. Lucy's right: It's not
about Jayson anymore. It's bigger than that.
I wish I had my phone to get a photo of this.
Seeing all the black armbands on the court
is rich, but seeing Coach standing open-
mouthed and speechless? Priceless.

Even though he's barefoot, Lex finishes
running the bleachers quicker than me. He
rejoins the team, and Dylan throws one of
the #BringBack45 bands toward him. Lex
avoids it like it's a bee coming to sting him.
When I join the team, I walk past, pick up the
band, then stand front and center of Coach. I
put it on, taking my sweet time about it. As I
walk toward my place in line, A.C. throws me
another band, and I put that on too. Unless
Lex is gonna play man-on-five defense, Coach
is faced with mass resistance. He'd better
surrender or go 2 and 20. His face turns redder
than the stripes on the Rebel flag hanging
from the rafters.

"You didn't really break up with Lucy, did you?" A.C. whispers. I don't answer.

"It's wrong that she got arrested, but look what it led to." He points at his armband.

Coach paces back and forth in front of us, eyes to the floor like he's looking for lost change. Nobody's making a sound. It's Sunday-church silent until Coach blows the whistle. "Stretching exercise, now!"

I look over Coach's shoulder. In the corner are Page and the two gray-suit guys. Maybe 45 isn't coming back, but I wonder if Coach is staying much longer.

I motion for A.C. to move closer. "If you don't bend with the times," I whisper, "I guess you break." I'm still hurting from Lex's knee, but when I stretch out my legs, I feel twenty feet tall.

WEDNESDAY MORNING
DECEMBER 21
Vestavia Hills High School

"Cody, wait up!" Ashley yells after me as I leave civics. "Slow down, Mr. Long Legs!"

I don't turn around. I'm deep into my phone, examining the crash and burn of #BringBack45. Like what happened to our season when Lex replaced Jayson, it's lost all momentum. Worse, there's even some mean pushback. This morning somebody posted a photo of a billboard that read "Diversity Means

Chasing Down the Last White Person." They used the hashtag "#TheNewWhiteGenocide" along with ours, so now all our sites are filled with hate speech, not hard facts.

"Cody, listen up!" Ashley tugs on the back of my game day jersey worn over my long-sleeved blue T-shirt. "How's Lucy? What happened to her was so wrong!"

"Her mom won't let her talk to me or text, so I don't know," I say softly.

"That's wrong too!"

"And it's all because she did something right," I say. "What good is it?" I show Ashley the vile photo.

She stares at the phone. "You want me to find out who did this? I bet that—"

"No, let it alone." I shake my head. People walk by us in the hallway cracking jokes like it's just another day, but it's not. Jayson, gone. Lucy, gone. Coach, here. Me, I don't matter.

"I'm not the only one," Ashley says. "Lots of people are upset about what happened."

"Not enough," I mumble. "I thought with it getting on the news and all . . ."

Ashley laughs and pokes her phone lightly into my chest. "Nobody watches the news. Everybody is too busy playing games. But I'm not playing. This isn't right. I won't shut up."

As the bell rings, making us both late for class, I say, "It will only make things worse."

"Hey, from what I know about you and Lucy, you two not together is as bad as it gets."

I bring up a picture of me and Lucy together from Homecoming. She's wearing that now-missing gold locket around her neck. Ashley smiles at it, but I frown. I bet Lucy's mom blames me for this. "I was following your advice, trying to do something good, and look at the result."

"Cody, who said the game was over?" Ashley says as she scoots off to second period. Maybe she's right: this might only be the first half of the game. If that's the case, I've got to organize a team and get ready to bring some serious skills in order to get Lucy back at school.

• • •

At practice, Coach drills us like an angry dentist, causing about as much hurt. I'm sure if he could, he would kick us all, except Lex, off the team. But I guess it's like a captain on a ship in the ocean faced with a mutiny: you either surrender to the mob or you die alone. Not that it's changed Coach's demeanor. He yells red hot at everybody, not only at the black players.

"Do it again!" Coach throws the ball so hard to Gerald that Gerald winces when he catches it. Coach is angry that we're losing, when he should be angry at the reason: himself. The only reason we're not getting blown out is that Dylan, A.C., and Gerald are making up the difference. "We have a game in two days, and you are not ready."

Dylan starts the ball down the court, scanning the second-string defense. Everybody gets into position as Dylan looks to make a pass. He rushes a pass to A.C., who soaks it up like a sponge. A.C. looks to Lex, who can't get open since I've got him covered like paper on rock, so A.C. puts up an off-balance jumper that hits off the backboard and into the net. I applaud inside.

"Run the plays, A.C.," Lex says, which means give him the ball more. Even though the players have changed, Coach won't change the offensive scheme. Lex is at center, a place he doesn't belong. The result: we're losing. But then again I'm used to that: I'm not a hero or a winner. I'm better than those things. I'm resilient.

When play resumes, Gerald passes to Lex, then sets a pick. Lex fakes right, then turns, but he gets tangled up in his new shoes and loses control of the ball. Gerald retrieves it, dribbles past Lex, performs a spin move that makes me dizzy, and lays it in. High fives from A.C. and Dylan, but Coach looks like he wants to give Gerald nothing but the back of his hand. Instead, he blows the whistle so it sounds as loud as a siren.

"What's wrong?" Gerald puts his hands on his hips, but I wish he'd put them over his ears to block out the trash Coach plans to talk.

"Good play, Gerald," Coach mumbles, like his mouth hurts. "Lex, switch with Cody."

I flip my jersey and join the four starters, an odd place for me. The second squad brings the ball down the court with Franklin at point. I cover second-string Lex, fight off a pick, reach out my arm, and block the pass. The ball jams hard into my right hand, then goes out of bounds. I want to cry in pain, but I bite my bottom lip instead.

"You okay?" Gerald asks.

I shake my right hand to show that I'm shaking it off. "I'm okay, just one finger."

"Which one?" Coach asks.

I show him. The middle one. Everybody laughs, even Coach. After everybody's done laughing, I head into the locker room to tape the finger. After I tape it, I open my locker and pull out my phone. I stare at the pic of Lucy and me from Homecoming, then scroll through the hundreds of others of us together. I lost at getting back number 45. I won't lose at getting back my #1.

After everybody dresses and exits, I head back toward the bleachers and continue my search for Lucy's locket. I clear my mind of

distraction because finding it is the only thing
that matters. This time, I find it right away.
But I don't know when I can return it. I pick
it up but don't put it in my pocket. Instead,
I hold it against my chest, knowing that
wherever Lucy is now, she'll be at the center of
my heart forever.

17

Vestavia Hills High School gym

Since it seems everything is cool on the team, Page and Coach decide to hold only the second pep rally of the season before our final home game before Christmas break. We're gonna need it because it's against Hoover High, so I guess we got our wish: number 45 is coming back.

In the locker room, Coach jingles loose change in his pockets. The team lines up so we can run into the gym before our classmates.

Everybody's in the bleachers—you don't get a choice about attending—except one person's not here: Lucy. She didn't have to spend time at juvie jail, but word is she's not coming back to school. Rumor is, Page expelled her pending some hearing after Christmas break. He'll get his hearing. He's gonna hear a lot, so I hope he has big ears.

"Let's do this!" Lex says, standing at the front of the line where starters stand, except A.C., Gerald, and Dylan casually slink to the back of the line next to me. "Let's go!"

We hear Brittany and the other cheerleaders chant their final *rah rah*, and then Page announces for everybody to "make some noise" for the Vestavia Hills Rebels. Little does he know that his team is about to live up to its name. Lex and the others exit the locker room like they were shot from a cannon. The crowd roars, but no one needs to wonder why the team is four players short.

"Ready?" I ask A.C. as I open Jayson's locker. He gave me the code. It's not empty. I pull out the contents. Each of us grabs an end.

And just like I'd planned with Ashley ahead of time, when A.C., Gerald, Dylan, and I emerge from the locker room, we hold up the big banner that reads #BringBackLucy. I've never heard a crowd so loud. Then up in the stands, Ashley, a bullhorn in hand, starts the chant.

"Bring back" *clap clap* "Lucy!" *clap clap*. I stand at the center of the gym, smiling ear to ear as the chants fill the gym, as loud as the roar of the tide of history. Mr. Austin was right: "Power to the people, right on!"

18

TUESDAY AFTERNOON
DECEMBER 27
Boutwell Auditorium

"Cody, you're in for Lex," Coach says, then claps his hands. The sound should wake me from the dream, except this is real. It's the first round in the Christmas Classics. Lex "Hack Master" fouled out with two minutes left, and we're five behind. "Run my plays and we'll win."

I nod like I agree, but once on the court, I sidle right over to A.C. "Showtime?"

He laughs, and we get into position. Gerald inbounds to Dylan, who starts the ball down the court, and I set up at the top of the key. Maybe the goons from Carver High figure I'm not a scoring threat because they've focused their attention elsewhere, so when I get the ball, I'm free to shoot. Instead, I hold on and wait for their center to defend, then comes the power forward. This lets A.C. streak toward the basketball, and I needle the pass to him. He inhales it and dunks. The crowd cheers, and while Coach no doubt frowns at the play, he's fine with the result.

Carver brings it up and they try to test me right away, not knowing there's really only one thing I learned from Coach. Their center gets the ball and heads toward the hoop. I hit the floor. The whistle blows, the ref calls the charge, and we take possession. Like we're in a loop, we run the same play, and the doofuses from Carver suffer another A.C. dunk attack.

Seconds tick down as Carver tries to crack us again, but just like we did around Jayson, the team pulls together and we're an iron wall they can't get through. The ball comes to their center, he tries around me again, but I won't give any ground. The ball goes up, and a three misses the mark and clangs off the backboard. I get into position, leap, and haul down the rebound. I look to pass but don't get a chance before a freckled arm slams down on my taped, aching finger. I bite my lip in pain.

I look at the scoreboard showing we need one to tie and two to win as I set myself at the foul line. In the stands, everybody wearing Rebel pride cheers, except Lucy, who is not there—or so everybody thinks. As I stand at the line, I touch Lucy's locket, which I'm wearing around my neck. My heart's beating with the game, and our place in the tournament is on the line.

Bam, goes my heart.

Bang, bang. I dribble the ball, finding my rhythm and setting myself. It is mind over matter: given everything that's gone on over the past few weeks, this game really doesn't matter, so I don't mind. I get my scattered mind out of the way and let my centered heart take over.

Swish. Tie game.

Bam, goes my heart.

Bang, bang, goes the ball.

Cheers or silence: it doesn't matter as I'm at the center—not of attention, but within myself.

Swish.

Check out all the titles in the

bOUNCE

Collection

STEP UP YOUR GAME

WELCOME TO THE DOJO

BODY SHOT
PATRICK JONES

SIDE CONTROL
PATRICK JONES

LEARN TO FIGHT, LEARN TO LIVE, AND LEARN TO FIGHT FOR YOUR LIFE.

HEAD KICK
PATRICK JONES

TRIANGLE CHOKE
PATRICK JONES

ABOUT THE AUTHOR

Patrick Jones is a former librarian for teenagers. He received lifetime achievement awards from the American Library Association and the Catholic Library Association in 2006. Jones has authored several titles for the following Darby Creek series: Turbocharged (2013); Opportunity (2013); The Dojo (2013), which won the YALSA Quick Picks for Reluctant Young Adult Readers award; The Red Zone (2014); The Alternative (2014); Bareknuckle (2014); and Locked Out (2015). He also authored *The Main Event: The Moves* and *Muscle of Pro Wrestling* (2013) which received the Chicago Public Library's Best of the Best Books list. While Patrick lives in Minneapolis, he still considers Flint, Michigan, his home. He can be found on the web at www.connectingya.com.